The Deaf Musicians

To my deaf father: Charles Louis Seeger, Jr.—P.S.

For Judy, Stretch, and Natalia—P.D.J.

For Mahamati, Scampi and Lady—thank you for the room and makeshift art table in Sydney.—R.G.C.

G. P. PUTNAM'S SONS
A division of Penguin Young Readers Group. Published by The Penguin Group. Penguin Group (USA) Inc., 375 Hudson Street, New York, NY 10014, U.S.A.
Penguin Group (Canada), 90 Eglinton Avenue East, Suite 700, Toronto, Ontario, Canada M4P 2Y3 (a division of Pearson Penguin Canada Inc.).
Penguin Books Ltd, 80 Strand, London WC2R 0RL, England. Penguin Ireland, 25 St. Stephen's Green, Dublin 2, Ireland (a division of Penguin Books Ltd.).
Penguin Group (Australia), 250 Camberwell Road, Camberwell, Victoria 3124, Australia (a division of Pearson Australia Group Pty Ltd).
Penguin Books India Pvt Ltd, 11 Community Centre, Panchsheel Park, New Delhi - 110 017, India.
Penguin Group (NZ), Cnr Airborne and Rosedale Roads, Albany, Auckland 1310, New Zealand (a division of Pearson New Zealand Ltd).
Penguin Books (South Africa) (Pty) Ltd, 24 Sturdee Avenue, Rosebank, Johannesburg 2196, South Africa.
Penguin Books Ltd, Registered Offices: 80 Strand, London WC2R 0RL, England.

The publisher does not have any control over and does not assume any responsibility for author or third-party websites or their content. Published simultaneously in Canada.
Manufactured in China by South China Printing Co. Ltd. Design by Marikka Tamura and Gunta Alexander. Text set in Angie Bold.
Library of Congress Cataloging-in-Publication Data
Seeger, Pete, 1919–
The deaf musicians / by Pete Seeger and Paul DuBois Jacobs ; illustrated by R. Gregory Christie.   p. cm.
Summary: Lee, a jazz pianist, has to leave his band when he begins losing his hearing, but he meets a deaf saxophone player in a sign language class and together they form
a snazzy new band. [1. Musicians—Fiction. 2. Deaf—Fiction. 3. Jazz—Fiction. 4. People with disabilities—Fiction.] I. Jacobs, Paul DuBois. II. Christie, Gregory, 1971– ill.
III. Title.   PZ7.S45153Dea 2006   [E]—dc22   2005026901   ISBN 0-399-24316-X
10 9 8 7 6 5 4 3 2 1
FIRST IMPRESSION

The Deaf Musicians

Story by **PETE SEEGER** and **PAUL DUBOIS JACOBS**

Illustrations by **R. GREGORY CHRISTIE**

G. P. PUTNAM'S SONS

Lee was a piano man. Every night, he would walk on stage at the jazz club to play his piano—snazzy style.
It went something like this:

Plink-a-plink BOMP plink-plink.
Yimba-timba-TANG—ZANG-ZANG.

But one night, Lee's bandmates noticed something.

"Lee, you didn't answer our notes, man. What's wrong?"

Lee was almost afraid to tell
them—he couldn't hear their notes.
He was losing his hearing.

His bandmates tried to cover for him, but Lee was just plain off. His music came out like this:

Ronk. Phip. Tonk.

It wasn't long before the bandleader noticed, too. "I'm sorry, Lee, but I'll have to let you go. Who will listen to a deaf musician?"

Poor Lee! He couldn't hear the trumpet go

Doodle-bop-bop, boo-bang-bing.

He couldn't hear the bass go

Bomba-bum, bomba-bum.

That night, riding home on the subway, Lee saw
an advertisement for a school for the deaf. *Maybe
I can learn how to do something new,* he thought.

The school turned out to be a very cool place. Lee loved sign language the best. To him, it looked like jazz.

He saw hands dancing with a doodle-bop-bop.

He saw fingers talking with a boo-bang-bing.

He saw bodies moving with a shish-shish-shoogle.

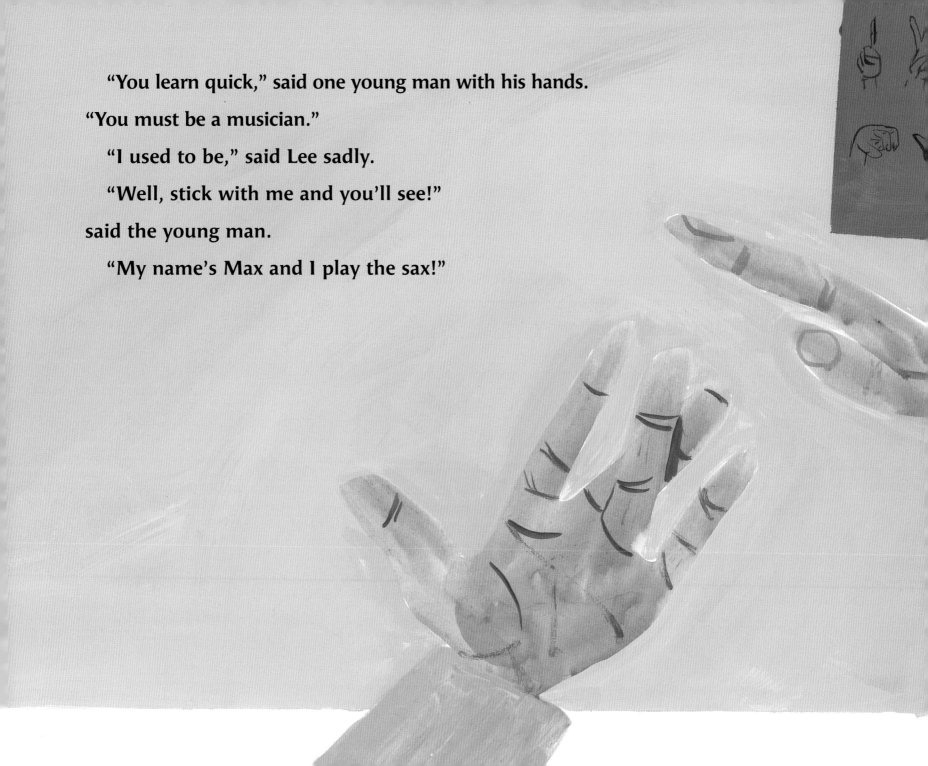

"You learn quick," said one young man with his hands.

"You must be a musician."

"I used to be," said Lee sadly.

"Well, stick with me and you'll see!"
said the young man.

"My name's Max and I play the sax!"

Riding the subway back and forth to school, Lee and Max rapped about their favorite jazz tunes. By using sign language, it was easy to talk over the racket of the subway cars and rush-hour crowds.

On one ride home, Lee and Max got to playing a song.
They found they could follow each other perfectly.

Lee played the notes of his piano—

Plink-a-plink-**BOMP**—

plink-

plink.

Yimba-timba-**TANG**-ZANG-ZANG.

Max played the notes of his sax—

Doodle-

bop-

bop,

boo-bang-bing.

Each musician heard
the music in his own mind.

It wasn't long before they were tossing tunes
back and forth every day.

One evening, a woman came up to them. "I know this song!"
she signed, fingers aflutter as if playing a stand-up bass.

Bomba-bum, bomba-bum.

"I like your style!" said Lee.

"Will you join our band?" asked Max.

The woman laughed. "I'd be honored. The name's Rose."

Soon the trio began to hold regular rehearsals in the subway.

But something was missing.

"We need a singer!" said Lee.

"I know just the one," smiled Rose.

Her friend Ellie was a sign-language interpreter, a translator
of sound. Ellie knew all the great jazz standards by heart.

OO-AH, BE-DOOP, BE-DOOP. OO-AH, YEAH!

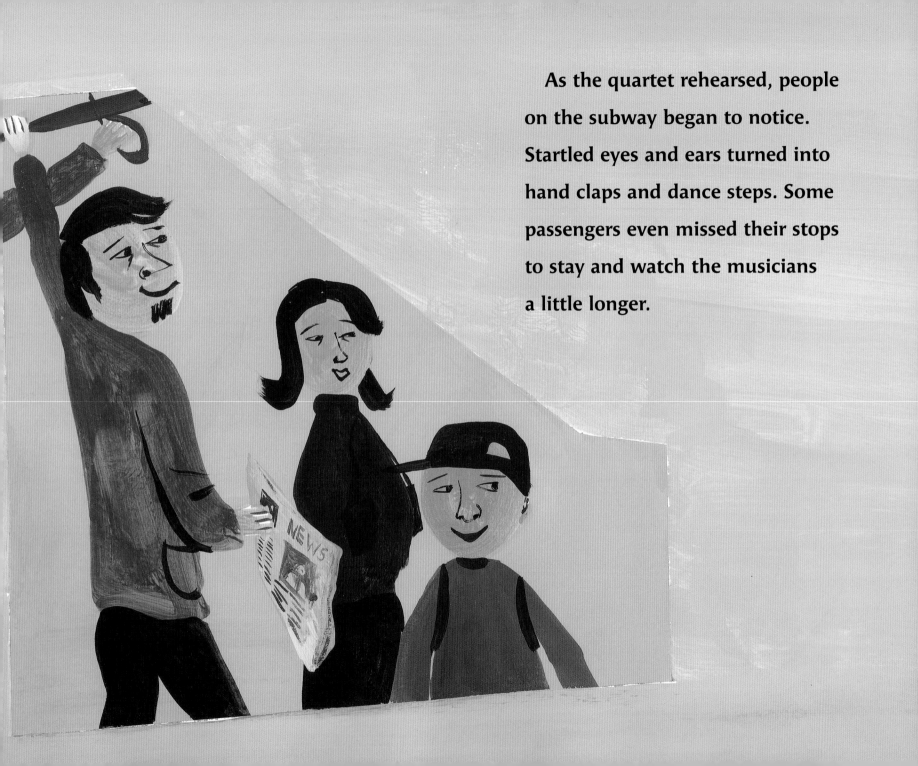

As the quartet rehearsed, people on the subway began to notice. Startled eyes and ears turned into hand claps and dance steps. Some passengers even missed their stops to stay and watch the musicians a little longer.

And Lee, who once thought his jazz life was over, found himself playing for audiences larger than ever before.

Night after night, Lee and his band would meet
in the subway to perform—

snazzy style.

One night, while they were playing, Lee's old bandleader appeared from out of the crowd. He gestured to Lee, "Your new band is fantastic!"

The two men shook hands. "Thanks," said Lee. "Remember when you asked me, 'Who will listen to a deaf musician?'

Afterword

Although I've never played with deaf musicians,
each year I participate in a music festival called
Clearwater's Great Hudson River Revival. One of
the festival's long-standing traditions is to have
a sign-language interpreter on every music
stage. It's a reminder of the power of music
even when it can't be heard.

I'm thankful to all the wonderful interpreters who've
joined me over the years in getting audiences to sing. After all, a chorus of
people working together is itself a kind of magic. I've seen this over and over
at concerts when the audience joins in on a song—the altos take one part, the
tenors take another, and other folks fill in between until there's a thunderous,
joyful sound—something much greater than the song that began.

The real music is in people joining together.

old Pete